For my own little sister, Jo Eddleston, with whom
I used to share a bedroom, with lots of love.

Pippa Goodhart

My Very Own Space is © Flying Eye Books 2017.

This is a second edition.

First published in 2017 by Flying Eye Books,
an imprint of Nobrow Ltd. 27 Westgate Street, London E8 3RL.

Text © Pippa Goodhart 2017. Illustrations © Rebecca Crane 2017.
Pippa Goodhart and Rebecca Crane have asserted their right under
the Copyright, Designs and Patents Act. 1988, to be identified
as the Author and Illustrator of this Work.

Published in the US by Nobrow (US) Inc.
Printed in Latvia on FSC® certified paper.

ISBN: 978-1-911171-12-6

Order from www.flyingeyebooks.com

MY VERY OWN SPACE

Pippa Goodhart   Rebecca Crane

Flying Eye Books
LONDON • NEW YORK

SHUSH!

I want to look at my book!

HELLO!

SPACE BUNNY

I want a space that's just for **ME.**

This space is MINE!

nothing is allowed over this line

OI! ALL OF YOU!

Go **AWAY** and play somewhere else!
This is **MY SPACE**!

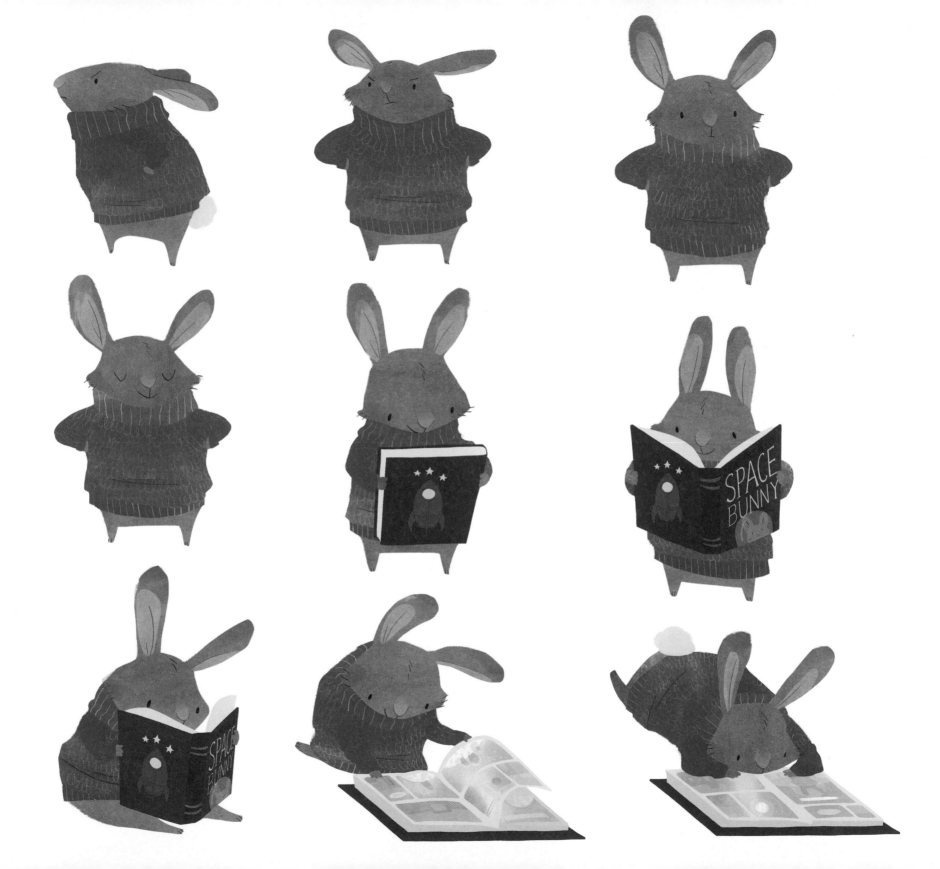

nothing is allowed over this line

nothing is allowed over this line

HEY!

Nothing and nobody
are allowed over the...

OH!

You can all come
into my space now.

ONE!
...TWO!
...THREE!

HA
HA
HA

HA
HA

SPACE
BUNNY

But there's still a bit of this space that's **just mine...**

...for some of the time.

Do you sometimes like to be alone?

Can you make a space that is just for you?

What things are fun to share
with friends and family?